I PROMISE

I PROMISE

Catherine Hernandez

Illustrations by
Syrus Marcus Ware

ARSENAL PULP PRESS
VANCOUVER

ARSENAL PULP PRESS
Suite 202 – 211 East Georgia St.
Vancouver, BC V6A 1Z6
Canada
arsenalpulp.com

The publisher gratefully acknowledges the support of the Canada Council for the Arts and the British Columbia Arts Council for its publishing program, and the Government of Canada, and the Government of British Columbia (through the Book Publishing Tax Credit Program), for its publishing activities.

Arsenal Pulp Press acknowledges the xʷməθkʷəy̓əm (Musqueam), Sḵwx̱wú7mesh (Squamish), and səl̓ilwəta?ł (Tsleil-Waututh) Nations, speakers of Hul'q'umi'num'/Halq'eméylem/hən̓q̓əmin̓əm̓ and custodians of the traditional, ancestral, and unceded territories where our office is located. We pay respect to their histories, traditions, and continuous living cultures and commit to accountability, respectful relations, and friendship.

This is a work of fiction. Any resemblance of characters to persons either living or deceased is purely coincidental.

Cover illustration by Syrus Marcus Ware

Printed and bound in Canada

Library and Archives Canada Cataloguing in Publication:
Title: I promise / Catherine Hernandez ; illustrations by Syrus Marcus Ware.
Names: Hernandez, Catherine, 1977- author. | Ware, Syrus Marcus, illustrator.
Identifiers: Canadiana (print) 20190100621 | Canadiana (ebook) 20190100737 | ISBN 9781551527796 (hardcover) | ISBN 9781551527802 (PDF)
Classification: LCC PS8615.E75 I2 2019 | DDC jC813/.6—dc23

To my two monkeys, Arden and Nazbah
To all of Dorothy's chirren, who love us for who we are
To my chosen family for choosing us in our journeys
together ... I hope you enjoy this promise fulfilled.
—CH

To Amélie for inspiring me every day, and to her and my
twin, Jessica, who together remind me every day that
anything is possible. To all the queer spawn and queer
kiddos out there, we love you!
—SMW

Mama?

Yes, kiddo?

You know Miracle from swim class? If she has two dads, where did she come from?

Well, Miracle came from a promise

that every child deserves a safe home,

a super comfy bed to sleep on,

and one more story before nighty-night.

What about Jun, who we met at the library?

If they have so many parents,

where did they come from?

Jun came from a promise to share and take turns

to make a family of twos

and threes

and fours

because some parents are awesome at building pillow forts

and some parents are better at flipping grilled cheeses

and wiping milk mustaches.

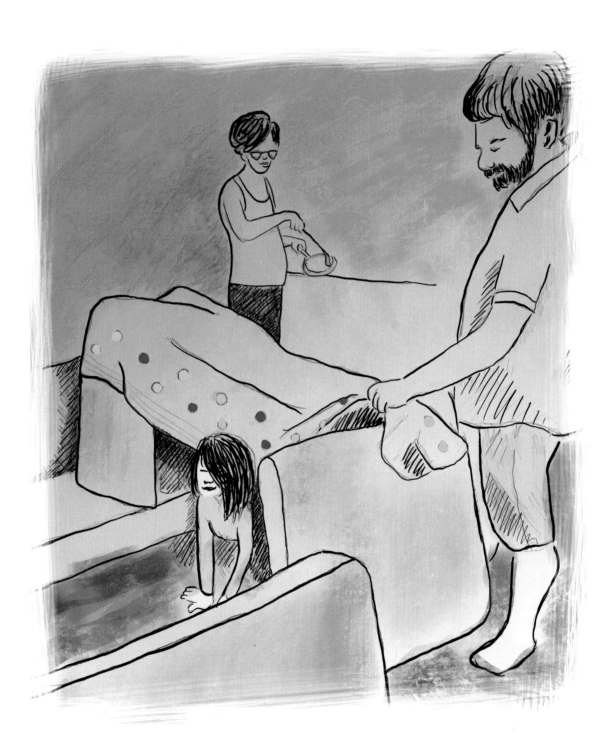

What about Cousin Frances?

Frances came from a promise

to teach a child to love her body,

to kiss every boo-boo,

and to put ice on her ouchies when kisses aren't enough.

And Cam?

From dance class?

What about him?

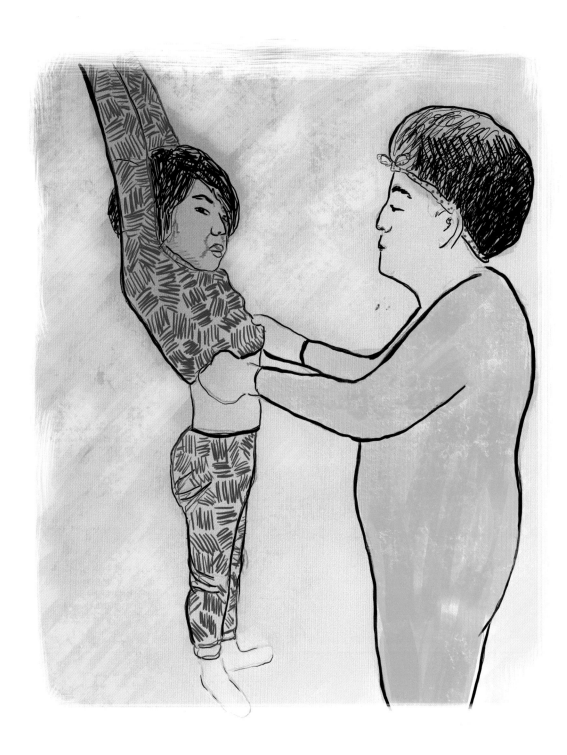

Cam came from a promise

that monsters do not belong under beds

and ladders sometimes feel like mountains,

especially when you're learning to

climb them for the first time.

And what about me?

If I only have one mama,

where did I come from?

You came from a promise

that pretend tea tastes better than real tea

and cardboard boxes are better than real cars.

You came from a promise

to clap for you when you learn something new

and to tuck you in really tight at night.

Mama, do you love me?

I'll always love you. I promise.

Photo: Dahlia Katz

SYRUS MARCUS WARE is a Vanier Scholar, visual artist, activist, curator, and educator. Syrus's work explores social justice frameworks and black activist culture. Syrus is a core-team member of both Black Lives Matter Toronto and Blackness Yes!/Blockorama. Syrus has won several awards, including the TD Diversity Award in 2017. Syrus is a PhD candidate at York University in the Faculty of Environmental Studies.

CATHERINE HERNANDEZ is a proud queer Filipina femme, Navajo wife, radical mother, award-winning author, and the artistic director of b current performing arts. She is the author of *Scarborough*, which won the 2015 Jim Wong-Chu Award; was shortlisted for the Toronto Book Award, Edmund White Award, and Trillium Book Award; was longlisted for Canada Reads; and was chosen for Queen's University's Queen's Reads program. She lives in Toronto.